For Mike and Kathryn Tickell — D. A.

For Carly — L. P.

THE DAM

David Almond

Illustrated by
Levi Pinfold

WALKER STUDIO
AN IMPRINT OF WALKER BOOKS LTD

He woke her early.

"Bring your fiddle," he said.

The day was dawning.

Into the valley they walked.

"This will be gone," he told her.

"And this."

"And this will be washed away."

"And this will never be seen again."

"And this will drown."

"And these can never live here again."

The dam was almost done.

"Archie Dagg the piper played here.

And Gracie Gray, she of the gorgeous voice."

"There were dances here.

There were parties."

"I came as a boy to hear them.

I brought you as a little girl. Remember?"

"Yes. Willy Taylor and his lovely violin.

The piccolo of Billy Ballantine."

"Bill Scott taught you the songs in there.

Remember his song book?"

"I hear them still."

"Take no notice.

There's no danger."

"Come inside now."

"Now play.

Play for all that are gone

and for all that are still to come.

Play, Kathryn, play."

"Sing, Daddy, sing.

Dance, Daddy, dance."

"Now this house. Now this one. Now this one."

They filled the houses with music.

The birds heard.

The beasts heard.

The earth heard.

The trees heard.

The ghosts heard.

The day was darkening.

Out of the valley they walked.

The dam was sealed.

The water rose.

This disappeared.

This was covered over.

This was drowned.

The lake is beautiful.

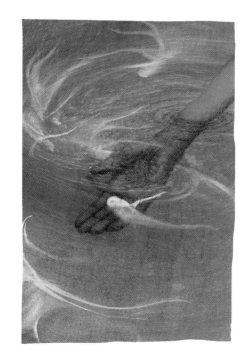

Behind the dam

Within the water the music stays,

Will never be gone.

We hear it when we walk the shores,

As we sail its satin surface,

As we fish its fertile waters,

As we paddle in its shallows,

As we lie beside it in the sun.

As we stare towards the stars.

The music rises.

It continues.

We hear it in the birds

And in the waves

And in the leaves

And in the grass.

We hear it when we are nearby

When we are far away

When we remember

When we dream.

The music is inside us.

It flows through all the dams in us.

It makes us play.

It makes us sing.

It makes us dance.

This is a true story. It was told to me by Mike and Kathryn Tickell. Kielder Water is the largest artificial lake in the UK. It is in North Northumberland, a wild and beautiful place, rich in folk music, story and legend. It was created in the late 70s and early 80s. A great dam was constructed  across the Kielder Valley, a place of farms, a school, several homesteads and a stretch of the Borders Counties Railway. The dam was completed in 1981. The valley took two years to fill with water. Kielder is now a place for walking, fishing, boating. It is part of the Northumberland International Dark Sky Park, the fourth largest in the world. It has an observatory, and an acclaimed collection of open-air art. Kathryn grew up to become one of the world's great folk musicians and composers. Mike is a singer and song-writer. The musical tradition thrives. Northumberland continues to be beautiful and wild.

First published 2018 by Walker Studio, an imprint of Walker Books Ltd, 87 Vauxhall Walk, London SE11 5HJ • 2 4 6 8 10 9 7 5 3 1 • Text © 2018 David Almond • Illustrations © 2018 Levi Pinfold • The right of David Almond and Levi Pinfold to be identified as author and illustrator respectively of this work has been asserted by them in accordance with the Copyright, Designs and Patents Act 1988 • This book has been typeset in Bookman Old Style • Printed in China • All rights reserved. No part of this book may be reproduced, transmitted or stored in an information retrieval system in any form or by any means, graphic, electronic or mechanical, including photocopying, taping and recording, without prior written permission from the publisher. • British Library Cataloguing in Publication Data: a catalogue record for this book is available from the British Library • ISBN 978-1-4063-0487-9 • **www.walker.co.uk**